Fables for the Frivolous

Fables for the Frivolous

by Guy Wetmore Carryl

CONTENTS

THE AMBITIOUS FOX AND THE UNAPPROACHABLE GRAPES

THE PERSEVERING TORTOISE AND THE PRETENTIOUS HARE

THE PATRICIAN PEACOCKS AND THE OVERWEENING JAY

THE ARROGANT FROG AND THE SUPERIOR BULL

THE DOMINEERING EAGLE AND THE INVENTIVE BRATLING

THE ICONOCLASTIC RUSTIC AND THE APROPOS ACORN

THE UNUSUAL GOOSE AND THE IMBECILIC WOODCUTTER

THE RUDE RAT AND THE UNOSTENTATIOUS OYSTER

THE URBAN RAT AND THE SUBURBAN RAT

THE IMPECUNIOUS CRICKET AND THE FRUGAL ANT

THE PAMPERED LAPDOG AND THE MISGUIDED ASS

THE VAINGLORIOUS OAK AND THE MODEST BULRUSH

THE INHUMAN WOLF AND THE LAMB SANS GENE

THE SYCOPHANTIC FOX AND THE GULLIBLE RAVEN

THE MICROSCOPIC TROUT AND THE MACHIAVELIAN FISHERMAN

THE CONFIDING PEASANT AND THE MALADROIT BEAR

Fables for the Frivolous

THE PRECIPITATE COCK AND THE UNAPPRECIATED PEARL

THE ABBREVIATED FOX AND HIS SCEPTICAL COMRADES

THE HOSPITABLE CALEDONIAN AND THE THANKLESS VIPER

THE IMPETUOUS BREEZE AND THE DIPLOMATIC SUN

THE AMBITIOUS FOX

AND

THE UNAPPROACHABLE GRAPES

A farmer built around his crop
  A wall, and crowned his labors
By placing glass upon the top
  To lacerate his neighbors,
    Provided they at any time
    Should feel disposed the wall to climb.

He also drove some iron pegs
  Securely in the coping,
To tear the bare, defenceless legs
  Of brats who, upward groping,
    Might steal, despite the risk of fall,
    The grapes that grew upon the wall.

One day a fox, on thieving bent,
  A crafty and an old one,
Most shrewdly tracked the pungent scent
  That eloquently told one
    That grapes were ripe and grapes were good
    And likewise in the neighborhood.

He threw some stones of divers shapes
  The luscious fruit to jar off:
It made him ill to see the grapes
  So near and yet so far off.
    His throws were strong, his aim was fine,
    But "Never touched me!" said the vine.

The farmer shouted, "Drat the boys!"
  And, mounting on a ladder,
He sought the cause of all the noise;
  No farmer could be madder,
    Which was not hard to understand
    Because the glass had cut his hand.

His passion he could not restrain,
  But shouted out, "You're thievish!"
The fox replied, with fine disdain,
  "Come, country, don't be peevish."
    (Now "country" is an epithet
    One can't forgive, nor yet forget.)

The farmer rudely answered back
  With compliments unvarnished,
And downward hurled the *bric-à-brac*
  With which the wall was garnished,
    In view of which demeanor strange,
    The fox retreated out of range.

"I will not try the grapes to-day,"
  He said. "My appetite is
Fastidious, and, anyway,
  I fear appendicitis."
    (The fox was one of the *élite*
    Who call it *site* instead of *seet*.)

The moral is that if your host
  Throws glass around his entry
You know it isn't done by most
  Who claim to be the gentry,
    While if he hits you in the head

You may be sure he's underbred.

"THE FOX RETREATED OUT OF RANGE" [*Page* 5

THE PERSEVERING TORTOISE

AND

THE PRETENTIOUS HARE

Once a turtle, finding plenty
  In seclusion to bewitch,
Lived a *dolce far niente*
  Kind of life within a ditch;
Rivers had no charm for him,
  As he told his wife and daughter,
"Though my friends are in the swim,
  Mud is thicker far than water."

One fine day, as was his habit,
  He was dozing in the sun,
When a young and flippant rabbit
  Happened by the ditch to run:
"Come and race me," he exclaimed,
  "Fat inhabitant of puddles.
Sluggard! You should be ashamed.
  Such a life the brain befuddles."

This, of course, was banter merely,
  But it stirred the torpid blood
Of the turtle, and severely
  Forth he issued from the mud.
"Done!" he cried. The race began,
  But the hare resumed his banter,
Seeing how his rival ran
  In a most unlovely canter.

Shouting, "Terrapin, you're bested!
  You'd be wiser, dear old chap,
If you sat you down and rested
  When you reach the second lap."
Quoth the turtle, "I refuse.
  As for you, with all your talking,

Sit on any lap you choose.
  I shall simply go on walking."

Now this sporting proposition
  Was, upon its face, absurd;
Yet the hare, with expedition,
  Took the tortoise at his word,
Ran until the final lap,
  Then, supposing he'd outclassed him,
Laid him down and took a nap
  And the patient turtle passed him!

Plodding on, he shortly made the
  Line that marked the victor's goal;
Paused, and found he'd won, and laid the
  Flattering unction to his soul.
Then in fashion grandiose,
  Like an after-dinner speaker,
Touched his flipper to his nose,
  And remarked, "Ahem! Eureka!"

And THE MORAL (lest you miss one)
  Is: There's often time to spare,
And that races are (like this one)
  Won not always by a hair.

THE PATRICIAN PEACOCKS

AND

THE OVERWEENING JAY

Once a flock of stately peacocks
  Promenaded on a green,
There were twenty-two or three cocks,
  Each as proud as seventeen,
And a glance, however hasty,
  Showed their plumage to be tasty;
Wheresoever one was placed, he
  Was a credit to the scene.

Now their owner had a daughter
  Who, when people came to call,
Used to say, "You'd reelly oughter
  See them peacocks on the mall."
Now this wasn't to her credit,
  And her callers came to dread it,
For the way the lady said it
  Wasn't *recherché* at all.

But a jay that overheard it
  From his perch upon a fir
Didn't take in how absurd it
  Was to every one but her;
When they answered, "You don't tell us!"
  And to see the birds seemed zealous
He became extremely jealous,
  Wishing, too, to make a stir.

As the peacocks fed together
  He would join them at their lunch,
Culling here and there a feather
  Till he'd gathered quite a bunch;
Then this bird, of ways perfidious,
  Stuck them on him most fastidious

Till he looked uncommon hideous,
  Like a Judy or a Punch.

But the peacocks, when they saw him,
  One and all began to haul,
And to harry and to claw him
  Till the creature couldn't crawl;
While their owner's vulgar daughter,
  When her startled callers sought her,
And to see the struggle brought her,
  Only said, "They're on the maul."

It was really quite revolting
  When the tumult died away,
One would think he had been moulting
  So dishevelled was the jay;
He was more than merely slighted,
  He was more than disunited,
He'd been simply dynamited
  In the fervor of the fray.

And THE MORAL of the verses
  Is: That short men can't be tall.
Nothing sillier or worse is
  Than a jay upon a mall.
And the jay opiniative
  Who, because he's imitative,
Thinks he's highly decorative
  Is the biggest jay of all.

THE ARROGANT FROG

AND

THE SUPERIOR BULL

Once, on a time and in a place
  Conducive to malaria,
There lived a member of the race
  Of *Rana Temporaria*;
    Or, more concisely still, a frog
    Inhabited a certain bog.

A bull of Brobdingnagian size,
  Too proud for condescension,
One morning chanced to cast his eyes
  Upon the frog I mention;
    And, being to the manner born,
    Surveyed him with a lofty scorn.

Perceiving this, the bactrian's frame
  With anger was inflated,
Till, growing larger, he became
  Egregiously elated;
    For inspiration's sudden spell
    Had pointed out a way to swell.

"Ha! ha!" he proudly cried, "a fig
  For this, your mammoth torso!
Just watch me while I grow as big
  As you--or even more so!"
    To which magniloquential gush
    His bullship simply answered "Tush!"

Alas! the frog's success was slight,

Which really was a wonder,
In view of how with main and might
He strove to grow rotunder!
And, standing patiently the while,
The bull displayed a quiet smile.

[Illustration: "HE STROVE TO GROW ROTUNDER"]

But ah, the frog tried once too oft
And, doing so, he busted;
Whereat the bull discreetly coughed
And moved away, disgusted,
As well he might, considering
The wretched taste that marked the thing.

THE MORAL: Everybody knows
How ill a wind it is that blows.

"HE STROVE TO GROW ROTUNDER"

THE DOMINEERING EAGLE

AND

THE INVENTIVE BRATLING

O'er a small suburban borough

Once an eagle used to fly,
Making observations thorough
  From his station in the sky,
And presenting the appearance
  Of an animated V,
Like the gulls that lend coherence
  Unto paintings of the sea.

Looking downward at a church in
  This attractive little shire,
He beheld a smallish urchin
  Shooting arrows at the spire;
In a spirit of derision,
  "Look alive!" the eagle said;
And, with infinite precision,
  Dropped a feather on his head.

Then the boy, annoyed distinctly
  By the freedom of the bird,
Voiced his anger quite succinctly
  In a single scathing word;
And he sat him on a barrow,
  And he fashioned of this same
Eagle's feather such an arrow
  As was worthy of the name.

Then he tried his bow, and, stringing
  It with caution and with care,
Sent that arrow singing, winging
  Towards the eagle in the air.
Straight it went, without an error,
  And the target, bathed in blood,
Lurched, and lunged, and fell to *terra*
  Firma, landing with a thud.

"Bird of freedom," quoth the urchin,
  With an unrelenting frown,
"You shall decorate a perch in
  The menagerie in town;
But of feathers quite a cluster
  I shall first remove for Ma:
Thanks to you, she'll have a duster
  For her precious *objets d'art*."

And THE MORAL is that pride is
  The precursor of a fall.
Those beneath you to deride is
  Not expedient at all.
Howsoever meek and humble
  Your inferiors may be,
They perchance may make you tumble,
  So respect them. Q. E. D.

THE ICONOCLASTIC RUSTIC

AND

THE APROPOS ACORN

Reposing 'neath some spreading trees,
  A populistic bumpkin
Amused himself by offering these
  Reflections on a pumpkin:
"I would not, if the choice were mine,
Grow things like that upon a vine,

For how imposing it would be
If pumpkins grew upon a tree."

Like other populists, you'll note,
  Of views enthusiastic,
He'd learned by heart, and said by rote
  A creed iconoclastic;
And in his dim, uncertain sight
Whatever wasn't must be right,
From which it follows he had strong
Convictions that what was, was wrong.

As thus he sat beneath an oak
  An acorn fell abruptly
And smote his nose: whereat he spoke
  Of acorns most corruptly.
"Great Scott!" he cried. "The Dickens!" too,
And other authors whom he knew,
And having duly mentioned those,
He expeditiously arose.

Then, though with pain he nearly swooned,
  He bathed his organ nasal
With arnica, and soothed the wound
  With extract of witch hazel;
And surely we may well excuse
The victim if he changed his views:
"If pumpkins fell from trees like that,"
He murmured, "Where would I be at?"

Of course it's wholly clear to you
  That when these words he uttered
He proved conclusively he knew
  Which side his bread was buttered;

And, if this point you have not missed,
You'll learn to love this populist,
The only one of all his kind
With sense enough to change his mind.

THE MORAL: In the early spring
A pumpkin-tree would be a thing
Most gratifying to us all,
But how about the early fall?

Fables for the Frivolous

"AN ACORN FELL ABRUPTLY"

THE UNUSUAL GOOSE

AND

THE IMBECILIC WOODCUTTER

A woodcutter bought him a gander,
  Or at least that was what he supposed,
As a matter of fact, 'twas a slander
  As a later occurrence disclosed;
For they locked the bird up in the garret
  To fatten, the while it grew old,
And it laid there a twenty-two carat
  Fine egg of the purest of gold!

There was much unaffected rejoicing
  In the home of the woodcutter then,
And his wife, her exuberance voicing,
  Proclaimed him most lucky of men.
"'Tis an omen of fortune, this gold egg,"
  She said, "and of practical use,
For this fowl doesn't lay any old egg,
  She's a highly superior goose."

Twas this creature's habitual custom,
  This laying of superfine eggs,
And they made it their practice to dust 'em
  And pack them by dozens in kegs:
But the woodcutter's mind being vapid
  And his foolishness more than profuse,
In order to get them more rapid
  He slaughtered the innocent goose.

He made her a gruel of acid
  Which she very obligingly ate,
And at once with a touchingly placid
  Demeanor succumbed to her fate.
With affection that passed the platonic
  They buried her under the moss,
And her epitaph wasn't ironic

In stating, "We mourn for our loss."

And THE MORAL: It isn't much use,
  As the woodcutter found to be true,
To lay for an innocent goose
  Just because she is laying for you.

THE RUDE RAT

AND

THE UNOSTENTATIOUS OYSTER

Upon the shore, a mile or more
  From traffic and confusion,
An oyster dwelt, because he felt
  A longing for seclusion;
Said he: "I love the stillness of
  This spot. It's like a cloister."
(These words I quote because, you note,
  They rhyme so well with oyster.)

A prying rat, believing that
  She needed change of diet,
In search of such disturbed this much-
  To-be-desired quiet.
To say the least, this tactless beast
  Was apt to rudely roister:
She tapped his shell, and called him--well,
  A name that hurt the oyster.

"I see," she cried, "you're open wide,
  And, searching for a reason,
September's here, and so it's clear
  That oysters are in season."
She smiled a smile that showed this style
  Of badinage rejoiced her,
Advanced a pace with easy grace,
  And *sniffed* the silent oyster.

The latter's pride was sorely tried,
  He thought of what he *could* say,
Reflected what the common lot
  Of vulgar molluscs *would* say;
Then caught his breath, grew pale as death,
  And, as his brow turned moister,
Began to close, and nipped her nose!
  Superb, dramatic oyster!

We note with joy that oi polloi,
  Whom maidens bite the thumb at,
Are apt to try some weak reply
  To things they should be dumb at.
THE MORAL, then, for crafty men
  Is: When a maid has voiced her
Contemptuous heart, don't think you're smart,
  But shut up--like the oyster.

THE URBAN RAT

AND

THE SUBURBAN RAT

A metropolitan rat invited
  His country cousin in town to dine:
The country cousin replied, "Delighted."
  And signed himself, "Sincerely thine."
The town rat treated the country cousin
        To half a dozen
        Kinds of wine.

He served him terrapin, kidneys devilled,
  And roasted partridge, and candied fruit;
In Little Neck Clams at first they revelled,
  And then in Pommery, *sec* and *brut*;
The country cousin exclaimed: "Such feeding
        Proclaims your breeding
        Beyond dispute!"

But just as, another bottle broaching,
  They came to chicken *en casserole*
A ravenous cat was heard approaching,
  And, passing his guest a finger-bowl,
The town rat murmured, "The feast is ended."
        And then descended
        The nearest hole.

His cousin followed him, helter-skelter,
  And, pausing beneath the pantry floor,
He glanced around at their dusty shelter
  And muttered, "This is a beastly bore.
My place as an epicure resigning,
        I'll try this dining
        In town no more.

"You must dine some night at my rustic cottage;
  I'll warn you now that it's simple fare:
A radish or two, a bowl of pottage,
  And the wine that's known as *ordinaire*,
But for holes I haven't to make a bee-line,
        No prowling feline
          Molests me there.

"You smile at the lot of a mere commuter,
  You think that my life is hard, mayhap,
But I'm sure than you I am far acuter:
  I ain't afraid of no cat nor trap."
The city rat could but meekly stammer,
        "Don't use such grammar,
          My worthy chap."

He dined next night with his poor relation,
  And caught dyspepsia, and lost his train,
He waited an hour in the lonely station,
  And said some things that were quite profane.
"I'll never," he cried, in tones complaining,
        "Try entertaining
          That rat again."

It's easy to make a memorandum
  About THE MORAL these verses teach:
De gustibus non est disputandum;
  The meaning of which Etruscan speech
Is wheresoever you're hunger quelling
        Pray keep your dwelling
          In easy reach.

THE IMPECUNIOUS CRICKET

AND

THE FRUGAL ANT

There was an ant, a spinster ant,
  Whose virtues were so many
That she became intolerant
  Of those who hadn't any:
She had a small and frugal mind
  And lived a life ascetic,
Nor was her temperament the kind
  That's known as sympathetic.

I skip details. Suffice to say
  That, knocking at her wicket,
There chanced to come one autumn day
  A common garden cricket
So ragged, poor, and needy that,
  Without elucidation,
One saw the symptoms of a bat
  Of several months' duration.

He paused beside her door-step, and,
  With one pathetic gesture,
He called attention with his hand
  To both his shoes and vesture.
"I joined," said he, "an opera troupe.
  They suddenly disbanded,
And left me on the hostel stoop,
  Lugubriously stranded.

"I therefore lay aside my pride
  And frankly ask for clothing."
"Begone!" the frugal ant replied.
  "I look on you with loathing.
Your muddy shoes have spoiled the lawn,
  Your hands have soiled the fence, too.
If you need money, go and pawn
  Your watch--if you have sense to."

THE MORAL is: Albeit lots
Of people follow Dr. Watts,
The sluggard, when his means are scant,
Should seek an uncle, not an ant!

THE PAMPERED LAPDOG

AND

THE MISGUIDED ASS

A woolly little terrier pup
  Gave vent to yelps distressing,
Whereat his mistress took him up
  And soothed him with caressing,
    And yet he was not in the least
    What one would call a handsome beast.

He might have been a Javanese,
  He might have been a Jap dog,
And also neither one of these,
  But just a common lapdog,

The kind that people send, you know,
Done up in cotton, to the Show.

At all events, whate'er his race,
  The pretty girl who owned him
Caressed his unattractive face
  And petted and cologned him,
    While, watching her with mournful eye,
    A patient ass stood silent by.

"If thus," he mused, "the feminine
  And fascinating gender
Is led to love, I, too, can win
  Her protestations tender."
    And then the poor, misguided chap
    Sat down upon the lady's lap.

Then, as her head with terror swam,
  "This method seems to suit you,"
Observed the ass, "so here I am."
  Said she, "Get up, you brute you!"
    And promptly screamed aloud for aid:
    No ass was ever more dismayed.

[Illustration: "SAID SHE, 'GET UP, YOU BRUTE YOU!'"]

They took the ass into the yard
  And there, with whip and truncheon,
They beat him, and they beat him hard,
  From breakfast-time till luncheon.
    He only gave a tearful gulp,
    Though almost pounded to a pulp.

THE MORAL is (or seems, at least,

To be): In etiquette you
Will find that while enough's a feast
 A surplus will upset you.
 Toujours, toujours la politesse, if
   The quantity be not excessive.

"SAID SHE, 'GET UP, YOU BRUTE YOU!'"

THE VAINGLORIOUS OAK

AND

THE MODEST BULRUSH

A bulrush stood on a river's rim,
  And an oak that grew near by
Looked down with cold *hauteur* on him,
  And addressed him this way: "Hi!"
The rush was a proud patrician, and
 He retorted, "Don't you know,
What the veriest boor should understand,
      That 'Hi' is low?"

This cutting rebuke the oak ignored.
  He returned, "My slender friend,
I will frankly state that I'm somewhat bored
  With the way you bow and bend."
"But you quite forget," the rush replied,
  "It's an art these bows to do,
An art I wouldn't attempt if I'd
      Such boughs as you."

"Of course," said the oak, "in my sapling days
  My habit it was to bow,
But the wildest storm that the winds could raise
  Would never disturb me now.
I challenge the breeze to make me bend,
  And the blast to make me sway."
The shrewd little bulrush answered, "Friend,
      Don't get so gay."

And the words had barely left his mouth

When he saw the oak turn pale,
For, racing along south-east-by-south,
  Came ripping a raging gale.
And the rush bent low as the storm went past,
  But stiffly stood the oak,
Though not for long, for he found the blast
        No idle joke.

* * * * * * * *

Imagine the lightning's gleaming bars,
  Imagine the thunder's roar,
For that is exactly what eight stars
  Are set in a row here for!
The oak lay prone when the storm was done,
  While the rush, still quite erect,
Remarked aside, "What under the sun
        Could one expect?"

And THE MORAL, I'd have you understand,
  Would have made La Fontaine blush,
For it's this: Some storms come early, and
        Avoid the rush!

THE INHUMAN WOLF

AND

THE LAMB SANS GENE

A gaunt and relentless wolf, possessed
  Of a quite insatiable thirst,

Once paused at a stream to drink and rest,
And found that, bound on a similar quest,
  A lamb had arrived there first.

The lamb was a lamb of a garrulous mind
  And frivolity most extreme:
In the fashion common to all his kind,
He cantered in front and galloped behind.
  And troubled the limpid stream.

"My friend," said the wolf, with a winsome air,
  "Your capers I can't admire."
"Go to!" quoth the lamb. (Though he said not where,
He showed what he meant by his brazen stare
  And the way that he gambolled higher.)

"My capers," he cried, "are the kind that are
  Invariably served with lamb.
Remember, this is a public bar,
And I'll do as I please. If your drink I mar,
  I don't give a tinker's ----."

He paused and glanced at the rivulet,
  And that pause than speech was worse,
For his roving eye a saw-mill met,
And, near it, the word which should be set
  At the end of the previous verse.

Said the wolf: "You are tough and may bring remorse,
  But of such is the world well rid.
I've swallowed your capers, I've swallowed your sauce,
And it's plain to be seen that my only course
  Is swallowing you." He did.

THE MORAL: The wisest lambs they are
  Who, when they're assailed by thirst,
Keep well away from a public bar;
For of all black sheep, or near, or far,
  The public bar-lamb's worst!

THE SYCOPHANTIC FOX

AND

THE GULLIBLE RAVEN

A raven sat upon a tree,
  And not a word he spoke, for
His beak contained a piece of Brie,
  Or, maybe, it was Roquefort:
    We'll make it any kind you please--
    At all events, it was a cheese.

Beneath the tree's umbrageous limb
  A hungry fox sat smiling;
He saw the raven watching him,
  And spoke in words beguiling.
    "*J'admire*," said he, "*ton beau plumage*."
    (The which was simply persiflage.)

Two things there are, no doubt you know,
  To which a fox is used:
A rooster that is bound to crow,
  A crow that's bound to roost,
    And whichsoever he espies

He tells the most unblushing lies.

"Sweet fowl," he said, "I understand
  You're more than merely natty,
I hear you sing to beat the band
  And Adelina Patti.
    Pray render with your liquid tongue
    A bit from 'Gotterdammerung.'"

This subtle speech was aimed to please
  The crow, and it succeeded:
He thought no bird in all the trees
  Could sing as well as he did.
    In flattery completely doused,
    He gave the "Jewel Song" from "Faust."

[Illustration: "'*J'ADMIRE*,' SAID HE, '*TON BEAU PLUMAGE*'"]

But gravitation's law, of course,
  As Isaac Newton showed it,
Exerted on the cheese its force,
  And elsewhere soon bestowed it.
    In fact, there is no need to tell
    What happened when to earth it fell.

I blush to add that when the bird
  Took in the situation
He said one brief, emphatic word,
  Unfit for publication.
    The fox was greatly startled, but
    He only sighed and answered "Tut."

THE MORAL is: A fox is bound

To be a shameless sinner.
And also: When the cheese comes round
  You know it's after dinner.
    But (what is only known to few)
    The fox is after dinner, too.

"'J'ADMIRE,' SAID HE, 'TON BEAU PLUMAGE'"

THE MICROSCOPIC TROUT

AND

THE MACHIAVELIAN FISHERMAN

A fisher was casting his flies in a brook,
  According to laws of such sciences,
With a patented reel and a patented hook
  And a number of other appliances;
And the thirty-fifth cast, which he vowed was the last
  (It was figured as close as a decimal),
Brought suddenly out of the water a trout
  Of measurements infinitesimal.

This fish had a way that would win him a place
  In the best and most polished society,
And he looked at the fisherman full in the face
  With a visible air of anxiety:
He murmered "Alas!" from his place in the grass,
  And then, when he'd twisted and wriggled, he
Remarked in a pet that his heart was upset
  And digestion all higgledy-piggledy.

"I request," he observed, "to be instantly flung
  Once again in the pool I've been living in."
The fisherman said, "You will tire out your tongue.
  Do you see any signs of my giving in?
Put you back in the pool? Why, you fatuous fool,
  I have eaten much smaller and thinner fish.
You're not salmon or sole, but I think, on the whole,
  You're a fairly respectable dinner-fish."

The fisherman's cook tried her hand on the trout
  And with various herbs she embellished him;
He was lovely to see, and there isn't a doubt
  That the fisherman's family relished him,
And, to prove that they did, both his wife and his kid
  Devoured the trout with much eagerness,
Avowing no dish could compare with that fish,
  Notwithstanding his singular meagreness.

And THE MORAL, you'll find, is although it is kind
  To grant favors that people are wishing for,
Still a dinner you'll lack if you chance to throw back
  In the pool little trout that you're fishing for;
If their pleading you spurn you will certainly learn
  That herbs will deliciously vary 'em:
It is needless to state that a trout on a plate
  Beats several in the aquarium.

THE CONFIDING PEASANT

AND

THE MALADROIT BEAR

A peasant had a docile bear,
  A bear of manners pleasant,
And all the love she had to spare
  She lavished on the peasant:
    She proved her deep affection plainly
    (The method was a bit ungainly).

The peasant had to dig and delve,
  And, as his class are apt to,
When all the whistles blew at twelve
  He ate his lunch, and napped, too,
    The bear a careful outlook keeping
    The while her master lay a-sleeping.

As thus the peasant slept one day,
  The weather being torrid,
A gnat beheld him where he lay
  And lit upon his forehead,
    And thence, like all such winged creatures,
    Proceeded over all his features.

The watchful bear, perceiving that
  The gnat lit on her master,
Resolved to light upon the gnat
  And plunge him in disaster;
    She saw no sense in being lenient
    When stones lay round her, most convenient.

And so a weighty rock she aimed
  With much enthusiasm:
"Oh, lor'!" the startled gnat exclaimed,
  And promptly had a spasm:
    A natural proceeding this was,
    Considering how close the miss was.

[Illustration: AND SO A WEIGHTY ROCK SHE AIMED]

Now by his dumb companion's pluck,
  Which caused the gnat to squall so,
The sleeping man was greatly struck
  (And by the bowlder, also).

In fact, his friends who idolized him
Remarked they hardly recognized him.

Of course the bear was greatly grieved,
  But, being just a dumb thing,
She only thought: "I was deceived,
  But still, I did hit *something!*"
    Which showed this masculine achievement
    Had somewhat soothed her deep bereavement.

THE MORAL: If you prize your bones
Beware of females throwing stones.

"AND SO A WEIGHTY ROCK SHE AIMED"

THE PRECIPITATE COCK

AND

THE UNAPPRECIATED PEARL

A rooster once pursued a worm
  That lingered not to brave him,
To see his wretched victim squirm
  A pleasant thrill it gave him;
He summoned all his kith and kin,
  They hastened up by legions,
With quaint, expressive gurgles in
  Their oesophageal regions.

Just then a kind of glimmering
  Attracting his attention,
The worm became too small a thing
  For more than passing mention:
The throng of hungry hens and rude
  He skilfully evaded.
Said he, "I' faith, if this be food,
  I saw the prize ere they did."

It was a large and costly pearl,
  Belonging in a necklace,
And dropped by some neglectful girl:
  Some people are so reckless!
The cock assumed an air forlorn,
  And cried, "It's really cruel.
I thought it was a grain of corn:
  It's nothing but a jewel."

He turned again to where his clan
  In one astounding tangle
With eager haste together ran
  To slay the helpless angle,
And sighed, "He was of massive size.
  I should have used discretion.

Too late! Around the toothsome prize
  A bargain-sale's in session."

The worm's remarks upon his plight
  Have never been recorded,
But any one may know how slight
  Diversion it afforded;
For worms and human beings are
  Unanimous that, when pecked,
To be the prey of men they far
  Prefer to being hen-pecked.

THE MORAL: When your dinner comes
  Don't leave it for your neighbors,
Because you hear the sound of drums
  And see the gleam of sabres;
Or, like the cock, you'll find too late
  That ornaments external
Do not for certain indicate
  A bona fide kernel.

THE ABBREVIATED FOX

AND

HIS SCEPTICAL COMRADES

A certain fox had a Grecian nose
  And a beautiful tail. His friends
Were wont to say in a jesting way
  A divinity shaped his ends.

The fact is sad, but his foxship had
  A fault we should all eschew:
He was so deceived that he quite believed
  What he heard from friends was true.

One day he found in a sheltered spot
  A trap with stalwart springs
That was cunningly planned to supply the demand
  For some of those tippet things.
The fox drew nigh, and resolved to try
  The way that the trap was set:
(When the trap was through with this interview
  There was one less tippet to get!)

The fox returned to his doting friends
  And said, with an awkward smile,
"My tail I know was *comme il faut*,
  And served me well for a while."
When his comrades laughed at his shortage aft
  He added, with scornful bow,
"Pray check your mirth, for I hear from Worth
  They're wearing them shorter now."

But one of his friends, a bookish chap,
  Replied, with a thoughtful frown,
"You know to-day the publishers say
  That the short tale won't go down;
And, upon my soul, I think on the whole,
  That the publishers' words are true.
I should hate, good sir, to part my fur
  In the middle, as done by you."

And another added these truthful words
  In the midst of the eager hush,

"We can part our hair 'most anywhere
  So long as we keep the brush."

THE MORAL is this: It is never amiss
  To treasure the things you've penned:
Preserve your tales, for, when all else fails,
  They'll be useful things--in the end.

THE HOSPITABLE CALEDONIAN

AND

THE THANKLESS VIPER

A Caledonian piper
  Who was walking on the wold
Nearly stepped upon a viper
  Rendered torpid by the cold;
By the sight of her admonished,
  He forbore to plant his boot,
But he showed he was astonished
  By the way he muttered "Hoot!"

Now this simple-minded piper
  Such a kindly nature had
That he lifted up the viper
  And bestowed her in his plaid.
"Though the Scot is stern, at least he
  No unhappy creature spurns,
'Sleekit, cowrin, tim'rous beastie,'"

Quoth the piper (quoting Burns).

This was unaffected kindness,
  But there was, to state the fact,
Just a slight *soupçon* of blindness
  In his charitable act.
If you'd watched the piper, shortly
  You'd have seen him leap aloft,
As this snake, of ways uncourtly,
  Bit him suddenly and oft.

There was really no excuse for
  This, the viper's cruel work,
And the piper found a use for
  Words he'd never learned at kirk;
But the biting was so thorough
  That although the doctors tried,
Not the best in Edinburgh
  Could assist him, and he died.

And THE MORAL is: The piper
  Of the matter made a botch;
One can hardly blame the viper
  If she took a nip of Scotch,
For she only did what he did,
  And *his* nippie wasn't small,
Otherwise, you see, he needed
  Not have seen the snake at all.

THE IMPETUOUS BREEZE

AND

THE DIPLOMATIC SUN

A Boston man an ulster had,
  An ulster with a cape that fluttered:
It smacked his face, and made him mad,
  And polyglot remarks he uttered:
    "I bought it at a bargain," said he,
    "I'm tired of the thing already."

The wind that chanced to blow that day
  Was easterly, and rather strong, too:
It loved to see the galling way
  That clothes vex those whom they belong to:
    "Now watch me," cried this spell of weather,
    "I'll rid him of it altogether."

It whirled the man across the street,
  It banged him up against a railing,
It twined the ulster round his feet,
  But all of this was unavailing:
    For not without resource it found him:
    He drew the ulster closer round him.

"My word!" the man was heard to say,
  "Although I like not such abuse, it's
Not strange the wind is strong to-day,
  It always is in Massachusetts.
    Such weather threatens much the health of
    Inhabitants this Commonwealth of."

The sun, emerging from a rift

Between the clouds, observed the victim,
And how the wind beset and biffed,
  Belabored, buffeted, and kicked him.
    Said he, "This wind is doubtless new here:
    'Tis quite the freshest ever blew here."

And then he put forth all his strength,
  His warmth with might and main exerted,
Till upward in its tube at length
  The mercury most nimbly spurted.
    Phenomenal the curious sight was,
    So swift the rise in Fahrenheit was.

The man supposed himself at first
  The prey of some new mode of smelting:
His pulses were about to burst,
  His every limb seemed slowly melting,
    And, as the heat began to numb him,
    He cast the ulster wildly from him.

"Impulsive breeze, the use of force,"
  Observed the sun, "a foolish act is,
Perceiving which, you see, of course.
  How highly efficacious tact is."
    The wondering wind replied, "Good gracious!
    You're right about the efficacious."

THE MORAL deals, as morals do,
  With tact, and all its virtues boasted,
But still I can't forget, can you,
  That wretched man, first chilled, then roasted?
    Bronchitis seized him shortly after,
    And that's no cause for vulgar laughter.

THE END

Printed in Great Britain
by Amazon.co.uk, Ltd.,
Marston Gate.